SOCCER TRIVIA

By Jon Marthaler

SportsZone

An Imprint of Abdo Publishing
abdopublishing.com

abdopublishing.com

Published by Abdo Publishing, a division of ABDO, PO Box 398166, Minneapolis, Minnesota 55439. Copyright © 2016 by Abdo Consulting Group, Inc. International copyrights reserved in all countries. No part of this book may be reproduced in any form without written permission from the publisher. SportsZone™ is a trademark and logo of Abdo Publishing.

Printed in the United States of America, North Mankato, Minnesota
082015
012016

Cover Photo: Elaine Thompson/AP Images
Interior Photos: Elaine Thompson/AP Images, 1, 4, 21; Nam Y. Huh/AP Images, 7; Bruno Luca/stf/AP Images, 9; John Super/AP Images, 11; Marcio Jose Sanchez/AP Images, 12; Eric Risberg/AP Images, 15; Jae C. Hong/AP Images, 17; Buenos Aires/El Grafico/AP Images, 18; Sean Dempsey/PA/AP Images, 23; Mark Lennihan/AP Images, 25; Alex Menendez/AP Images, 27; AP Images, 28, 32, 35, 37; Nick Wass/AP Images, 30; Frank Augstein/AP Images, 38; Bippa/AP Images, 41; Eric Draper/AP Images, 43

Editor: Patrick Donnelly
Series Designer: Jake Nordby

Library of Congress Control Number: 2015945863

Cataloging-in-Publication Data
Marthaler, Jon.
 Soccer trivia / Jon Marthaler.
   p. cm. -- (Sports trivia)
ISBN 978-1-68078-006-2 (lib. bdg.)
Includes bibliographical references and index.
1. Soccer--Miscellanea--Juvenile literature.   2. Sports--Miscellanea--Juvenile literature.   I. Title.
796.334--dc23

                                                    2015945863

CONTENTs

Soccer is known as the Beautiful Game. It is by far the most popular sport around the world. It is played from Argentina and Australia in the south to Norway and Iceland in the north. The men's World Cup is the biggest sporting event in the world. It features the best national teams. Professional club teams play in cities around the world. Fans pack stadiums each weekend from Sao Paolo to Seattle to Sydney. Millions more tune in to watch matches on television. In the United States, soccer becomes more popular every year. How well do you know the Beautiful Game? Check out this book and test your soccer knowledge!

*All statistics and answers are current through July 2015.

CHAPTER 1

ROOKIE

Q Who scored the most career goals in Major League Soccer (MLS) and for the US Men's National Team?

A Landon Donovan scored 144 MLS goals in his career. He played for the San Jose Earthquakes (2001–04) and the Los Angeles Galaxy (2005–14). He also scored 57 goals for the United States. He retired in 2014. MLS named its Most Valuable Player (MVP) trophy after Donovan.

Q Who scored a hat trick for the United States in the 2015 Women's World Cup final?

A Carli Lloyd scored three goals as the Americans routed Japan 5–2 in Vancouver, Canada. Lloyd's third goal—

Landon Donovan, *left*, celebrates a goal with teammate DaMarcus Beasley.

from just beyond the midfield stripe—gave the United States a 4–0 lead just 16 minutes into the game.

Q When did MLS begin?

A The top league in the United States began play in 1996. But MLS is not the first professional US soccer league. The North American Soccer League (NASL) drew huge crowds at its peak of popularity. The NASL started play in 1968 and ended in 1984.

Q Which country has won the most World Cups?

A Brazil has won the men's World Cup five times (1958, 1962, 1970, 1994, and 2002). Italy and Germany have won four times each. The United States has won the Women's World Cup three times—1991, 1999, and 2015.

Q When was the men's World Cup held in the United States?

A It made its US debut in 1994. Many people thought soccer was not popular enough in the United States. They expected the tournament to fail. But more than

3.5 million tickets were sold. That was more than any other World Cup. More than 94,000 people watched Brazil beat Italy for the championship. The final was held at the Rose Bowl in Pasadena, California.

Q **What happens after a player is given a red card?**

A A player who is given a red card is thrown out of the game and cannot be replaced. Players receive red cards for committing dangerous fouls or for unsportsmanlike behavior. A foul that keeps the other team from scoring a goal also can draw a red card. Referees give yellow cards for cautions. Players given two yellow cards in a match are also shown a red card and ejected.

Q **Which English star played for the Los Angeles Galaxy from 2007 to 2012?**

A David Beckham became famous while playing for Manchester United and Real Madrid. Those are two of the most popular teams in the world. In 2007 the midfielder moved to the United States to play. His arrival led to a lot of attention for the Los Angeles Galaxy. His team won the Supporters' Shield in 2010 and 2011. It also won the MLS Cup in 2011 and 2012.

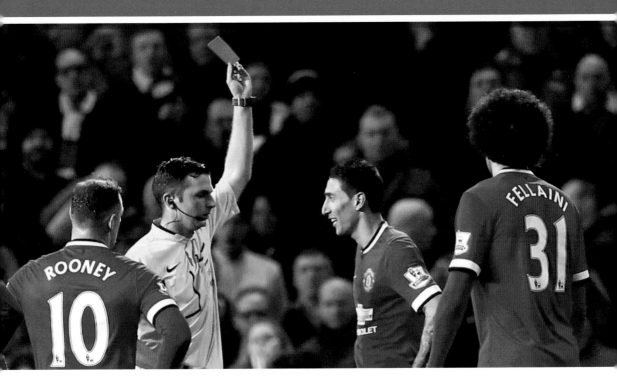

Q Which five soccer leagues are Europe's most well-known?

A The Premier League in England, La Liga in Spain, the Bundesliga in Germany, Serie A in Italy, and Ligue 1 in France make up the "Big Five." The majority of the most popular teams and most famous players in the world play in these five leagues. Fans from around the world watch their games.

US forward Abby Wambach, *20*, heads home a goal against France in the 2011 Women's World Cup.

Q Which English team has won the most top-division league titles?

A Manchester United has won the league title in England's top division 20 times. Liverpool is second with 18 championships. England's top division is called the

Premier League. It replaced the old Football League First Division in 1992–93. The Football League First Division had been around since the late 1800s. In the Premier League era, Manchester United has won 13 titles.

Q **Why does the goalkeeper wear a different color jersey than the rest of the team?**

A Goalkeepers are the only players allowed to touch the ball with their hands. Goalies' unique uniforms help the referees tell them apart from the other players.

WHO IS THE US WOMEN'S NATIONAL TEAM'S ALL-TIME LEADING SCORER?

Abby Wambach scored her record-setting 159th goal in 2013. And she is still playing. Fellow US striker Mia Hamm held the previous record. She scored 158 international goals between 1987 and 2004. Wambach and Hamm won an Olympic gold medal together in 2004.

CHAPTER 2

VETERAN

Q **Who scored the goal that clinched the 1999 Women's World Cup title?**

A US defender Brandi Chastain was the hero that day. The 1999 Women's World Cup final featured the United States and China. The game was scoreless through 90 minutes. Nobody scored in the two 15-minute extra time periods either. It came down to a penalty kick shootout. Chastain's goal clinched a 5–4 shootout victory. Following her goal, Chastain whipped off her jersey in celebration. It was the defining image of the first Women's World Cup played in the United States.

Brandi Chastain celebrates after winning the 1999 Women's World Cup.

Who has scored more goals than any other player in the Spanish League?

A Lionel Messi has scored more than 400 goals in his career with Barcelona. That is the most in the team's history. Club soccer teams play in various competitions. Messi has scored more than 280 goals (and counting) in league play. He is the all-time leading scorer in La Liga. He also has been a star for Barcelona in various tournaments. The European Champions League is the biggest tournament. Messi is the only player to have led the Champions League in scoring four years in a row. He did that from 2008–09 to 2011–12.

Q **How late was Landon Donovan's goal against Algeria that allowed the US Men's National Team to advance to the knockout round at the 2010 World Cup?**

A Donovan scored in the 91st minute. The goal set off a wild celebration among US fans. The United States beat Algeria 1–0 in the team's final game of the group stage of the tournament. A draw or loss would have ended the Americans' tournament.

Q **Who has played in the most Women's World Cup matches?**

A Kristine Lilly played 30 matches for the United States in five Women's World Cups. This is the most of any player, woman or man. No other player has more than 25 appearances at the World Cup.

Q **Which country has finished second in the most World Cups without ever winning the tournament?**

A The Netherlands finished second three times, in 1974, 1978, and 2010. It also

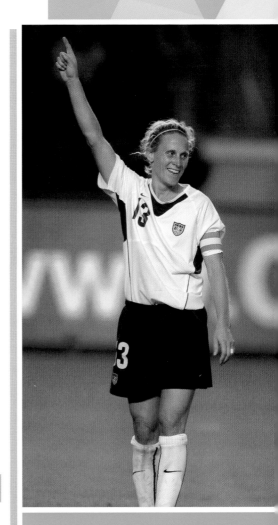

Kristine Lilly

Argentina's Diego Maradona, *left*, scores the "Hand of God" goal over England's Peter Shilton in the 1986 World Cup.

finished third in 2014 and fourth in 1998. Two losses—in 1978 to Argentina and in 2010 to Spain—came in extra time.

Q **Which player has won the most World Cups?**

A Pelé won the World Cup three times with Brazil. He won championships in 1958, 1962, and 1970. Including his games in the 1966 World Cup, he scored 12 goals. This is the fifth-most of all time.

Q **Who is the youngest player to score a goal in MLS history?**

A Freddy Adu was only 14 years old when he scored his first MLS goal. On April 17, 2004,

WHICH LEGENDARY PLAYER SCORED A GOAL KNOWN AS THE "HAND OF GOD"?
Diego Maradona scored both goals in a 2–1 Argentina win over England at the 1986 World Cup. Maradona's first goal came when he jumped up and punched the ball over the goalkeeper. The referee did not see him touch the ball with his hand. So the goal was allowed. After the game, Maradona said the goal was scored "a little with the head of Maradona and a little with the hand of God."

Adu scored for DC United in a 3–2 loss to the New York/New Jersey MetroStars. He is the only 14-year-old to ever play in MLS.

Q Who stopped the most shots in a single World Cup match?

A US goalkeeper Tim Howard made 16 saves against Belgium in the 2014 World Cup. It was the most saves in a World Cup game since FIFA began keeping track of saves in 1966. The United States still lost 2–1, though.

Q Which soccer team is nicknamed the Socceroos?

A The Australia men's national team is known as the "Socceroos." The nickname was made up by a journalist in 1967. The Australia women's national team is known as the "Matildas." Until 1995, the women's team was called the "Female Socceroos."

US keeper Tim Howard makes one of his 16 saves against Belgium in the 2014 World Cup.

How does the US Open Cup differ from the MLS Cup?

A The MLS Cup is for MLS teams only. However, any US team can enter the US Open Cup. Amateur teams play in a qualifying tournament. The winners play against professional teams in a knockout tournament. MLS teams also enter the tournament. The last time a non-MLS team won was in 1999. The Rochester Rhinos were in the second division that year. But they beat four MLS teams on their way to the title.

Which is the only Premier League team to go through an entire season without a loss?

A In 2003–04, Arsenal went an entire season without losing. The team was nicknamed "The Invincibles" for the feat. It won 26 games and had 12 ties (also called draws). At three points per victory and one point per draw, Arsenal finished with 90 points. That was 11 points ahead of second-place Chelsea, one of its main rivals. The next year, Chelsea set a Premier League record with 95 points. But Chelsea's results included one loss.

CHAPTER 3

CHAMPION

Q Who scored the goal known as the "Shot Heard Round the World" for the United States in 1989?

A Paul Caligiuri officially returned the United States to the global stage with his big goal. The US team was in Trinidad and Tobago. It needed a win to qualify for its first World Cup since 1950. The team also needed to prove itself a worthy host of the 1994 World Cup. Caligiuri did the trick. His goal gave the United States a 1–0 win. The Americans went to the 1990 World Cup in Italy and have not missed the tournament since.

Paul Caligiuri, *second from left*, celebrates with his US teammates in 1989.

Which stadium has hosted four consecutive US victories in World Cup qualifiers against Mexico?

A MAPFRE Stadium in Columbus, Ohio, has been the site of the last four US-Mexico World Cup qualifiers. The streak started in 2001 and continued through 2013. In each of the four games, the United States won 2–0. US fans refer to these games as "Dos a Cero." That is the Spanish translation for the final score in each game.

Q **Five MLS teams still have the same name as they did in 1996. Which ones are they?**

A DC United, the Los Angeles Galaxy, the Colorado Rapids, the Columbus Crew, and the New England Revolution have kept their original names. Three other teams remain from the original 10. However, they have since changed their names. FC Dallas was originally the Dallas Burn, Sporting Kansas City was the Kansas City Wiz (and later the Wizards), and Red Bull New York began as the New York/New Jersey MetroStars.

Q Which US player outscored all opposing teams by herself in 2012?

A Striker Alex Morgan scored 28 goals for the United States in 2012. She also had 21 assists. That year US opponents combined for just 21 goals and 12 assists in 32 games. Morgan was the first US women's player to have at least 20 goals and 20 assists in one year since Mia Hamm in 1998.

Alex Morgan

Q Which Spanish teams play in "El Clásico" games?

A Any game between Barcelona and Real Madrid is called "El Clásico." Barcelona and

Real Madrid are almost always the best two teams in Spain. "El Clásico" translates to "The Classic" in English. The two teams have combined to win 55 La Liga championships. This includes 26 of the last 31 La Liga titles.

Q **What are the two soccer seasons called in Liga MX, the Mexican top league?**

A Mexican teams play an *apertura* (opening) tournament from July to December. Then they play a *clausura* (closing) tournament from January to May. Each tournament crowns a champion. This means there are two champions per year in Liga MX.

Q **Which is the only country not to qualify for the knockout round while hosting the World Cup?**

A South Africa fell short when it hosted the World Cup in 2010. In group play it won one game, tied one, and lost one.

WHICH OPPONENT DID THE UNITED STATES BEAT IN A GAME KNOWN AS THE "MIRACLE ON GRASS"?

The United States beat England 1–0 at the 1950 World Cup. It was one of the biggest upsets in the history of the tournament. England was a 3-to-1 favorite to win the World Cup that year. The US team was made up of semi-professional players who had other jobs. They were a 500-to-1 shot to win. Joe Gaetjens scored the game's only goal.

The team finished third in its group. This meant that it did not move on to the knockout round that decides the champion.

Q Who is the only player to have won the MLS MVP Award and the MLS Goalkeeper of the Year Award in the same year?

A Tony Meola won both of these awards in 2000. He had 16 shutouts that year for the Kansas City Wizards. Kansas City won the league championship that year, and Meola was also named the MLS Cup MVP.

Q Which US Women's National Team players were known as the "Fab Five"?

A Mia Hamm, Julie Foudy, Kristine Lilly, Brandi Chastain, and Joy Fawcett made up the Fab Five. They played together for the United States between 1991 and 2004. They won the Women's World Cup in 1991 and 1999. They also won Olympic gold medals in 1996 and 2004. They had 1,330 combined appearances for the United States.

Estadio Azteca is packed for a 1970 World Cup game between Mexico and the Soviet Union.

Q Which is the largest soccer stadium in North America?

A The Estadio Azteca in Mexico City seats 95,500 people. It is the home stadium of the Mexico National Team. Club America, one of the best teams in the Mexican league, also plays its home games there. The stadium hosted the World Cup championship game in 1970 and 1986. It is the only stadium to have hosted more than one.

Q **Which team has won the Bundesliga more than any other team?**

A Bayern Munich has a record 25 Bundesliga titles. That is the title for the top league in Germany. It has also won the DFB-Pokal 17 times. The DFB-Pokal is the Germany-wide knockout cup competition. Bayern Munich's 25 league wins and 17 cup wins are far more than any other German team.

CHAPTER 4

HALL OF FAMER

Q Which Brazilian superstar led the New York Cosmos between 1975 and 1977?

A Pelé was the biggest star to play in the NASL in the 1970s. New York convinced him to come out of retirement to play in 1975. Huge crowds attended Cosmos matches wherever they played. Everybody wanted to see Pelé. New York won the NASL championship in his final season.

Q Who scored an own goal for Colombia in the 1994 World Cup, leading to a 2–1 victory for the United States?

Pelé, *right*, makes his debut with the New York Cosmos on June 15, 1975.

A Andres Escobar deflected a pass into his own net. This goal helped the United States upset Colombia. The Colombians came into the tournament as one of the favorites to win. But the loss kept Colombia out of the knockout round. Nine days later, after Escobar had returned home, he was shot and killed by a man who was angry about the outcome of the game.

Q **Which player did Real Madrid acquire for a $132 million transfer fee in 2013?**

A Real Madrid paid 100 million euros—about $132 million—to Premier League team Tottenham Hotspur for winger Gareth Bale. It smashed the record for the most money paid for a player. The previous record was also held by Real Madrid. It paid a transfer fee of 94 million euros to Manchester United for Portuguese striker Cristiano Ronaldo in 2009.

Real Madrid opened the bank vault to land former Tottenham Hotspur star Gareth Bale in 2013.

Miroslav Klose, *right,* **scores against Costa Rica during the 2006 World Cup.**

Q **Who scored to clinch the 2012 English Premier League title for Manchester City?**

A Sergio "Kun" Aguero scored in the fifth minute of stoppage time of Manchester City's last game of the season. That goal gave his team a 3–2 win to clinch the league title. If the game had ended 2–2, Manchester United would have won the championship instead. It was Manchester City's first league title since 1968.

Q Who are the only two women who have played in the finals of the World Cup for both cricket and soccer?

A Clare Taylor of England and Ellyse Perry of Australia are the versatile athletes. Taylor played four times for England at the 1995 Women's World Cup. Perry played twice for Australia at the 2011 Women's World Cup. Both have won the Women's Cricket World Cup as well.

WHO HAS SCORED THE MOST GOALS IN WORLD CUP HISTORY?

German striker Miroslav Klose has scored 16 goals in the World Cup. He played in four World Cups: 2002, 2006, 2010, and 2014. His final goal came against Brazil in the 2014 semifinals. Germany beat Brazil 7–1 in that game.

Q Which is the only team to play an entire World Cup without giving up a goal?

A Switzerland won its group at the 2006 World Cup. It qualified for the knockout

round by tying France 0–0 and then beating both Togo and South Korea 2–0. In the knockout round, the Swiss tied Ukraine 0–0, but they lost in a penalty kick shootout. They allowed zero goals but did not even finish among the top eight teams.

Q Where is the original World Cup trophy?

A Nobody knows. The Jules Rimet Trophy was made for the first World Cup in 1930. In 1970 it was given to Brazil for winning the World Cup three times. Thieves broke into the Brazilian soccer headquarters in 1983. They stole the original trophy from the trophy case. It has not been seen since.

Q Which team has gone the longest without being relegated from England's first division?

A Arsenal has the longest streak. Every year the worst three teams in the top division in England are relegated. That means they are sent down to the second division. The three best teams from the second division take their

England captain Bobby Moore receives the Jules Rimet Trophy from Queen Elizabeth after the 1966 World Cup final.

place. Arsenal has finished above the bottom three every year since 1919.

Q Which team won the Champions League in 2014 and has won it more than any other team?

A Real Madrid has won the Champions League 10 times. The Spanish team won five times in a row between 1956 and 1960. These were the first five times the tournament was held. The team also won in 1966 but then did not win again until 1998. Three more titles came in 2000, 2002, and 2014.

Q Who scored the first goal in MLS history?

A On April 6, 1996, Eric Wynalda scored the first MLS goal. It gave the San Diego Clash a 1–0 win over DC United. It was later named the Goal of the Season in 1996. Wynalda is now a popular soccer announcer on TV.

Q Which Italian team has won the most Serie A titles and was also kicked out of the league in 2006 for fixing games?

A Juventus has won the Italian league a record 31 times. In 2006, though, investigators caught the team's general manager arranging friendly referees for his team's matches. Juventus had to forfeit the 2005 and 2006 league titles. Juventus also had to play in the second division in 2007.

TRIVIA QUIZ

1 **How many referees are on the field for a typical soccer game?**

a. Two referees—one on each side of the field

b. Three referees—one center referee and two assistants

c. Three referees—one main referee and two goal judges

d. Four referees—two on each side of the field and two in the middle

2 **What is the name of Seattle's MLS team?**

a. United

b. Sounders

c. Seahawks

d. Republic

3 **Who has won the most FIFA Women's Player of the Year Awards?**

a. Mia Hamm, USA

b. Abby Wambach, USA

c. Birgit Prinz, Germany

d. Marta, Brazil

4 **Who scored the winning goal in the 2014 World Cup Final?**

a. Mario Göetze

b. Lionel Messi

c. Miroslav Klose

d. Bastian Schweinsteiger

5 Which of these clubs has Cristiano Ronaldo never played for?

a. Manchester United

b. Sporting Lisbon

c. Real Madrid

d. Chelsea

6 Which of these pairs of teams joined MLS as expansion teams in 2015?

a. Orlando City and New York City FC

b. Chivas USA and Real Salt Lake

c. Orlando City and Los Angeles FC

d. Minnesota United and New York City FC

7 Where is the English FA Cup Final held?

a. MetLife Stadium, New Jersey

b. Old Trafford, Manchester

c. Wembley Stadium, London

d. England Park, London

8 Who was the first American to play in the Premier League in England?

a. Landon Donovan

b. John Harkes

c. Tab Ramos

d. Brian McBride

9 Which of these pairs of European soccer teams do not play in the same city?

a. Arsenal and Tottenham

b. AC Milan and Internazionale

c. Barcelona and Villareal

d. Liverpool and Everton

10 Who, at age 18, was the youngest US Women's World Cup player ever?

a. Tiffany Roberts

b. Alex Morgan

c. Mia Hamm

d. Holly Manthei

*Answers on page 47

GLOSSARY

extra time
Additional 15-minute periods added to a game when it is still tied at the end of 90 minutes.

own goal
A goal that is accidentally scored by a player against his own team.

penalty kick
An unguarded kick from the penalty spot, which is 12 yards away from the goal. The shooter goes one-on-one against the goalkeeper.

relegated
Moved down to a different league division. In many world soccer leagues, the teams that finish at the bottom of the standings are relegated to a lower division, while the best teams in the lower division are promoted to the higher division.

shutout
Going through a whole game without giving up a goal to the other team. This is sometimes also called a "clean sheet."

stoppage time
Time added at the end of each half to account for stoppages in play. This is also known as "injury time."

transfer fee
The money that one team will pay another team to trade, or transfer, a player.

FOR MORE INFORMATION

Books

Jankowski, Emily. *Soccer's Greatest Records*. New York: PowerKids Press, 2015.

Jökulsson, Illugi. *Alex Morgan*. New York: Abbeville Kids, 2015.

Rausch, David. *Major League Soccer*. Minneapolis, MN: Bellwether Media, Inc., 2015.

Websites

To learn more about Sports Trivia, visit **booklinks.abdopublishing.com**. These links are routinely monitored and updated to provide the most current information available.

Answers

1.	b	6.	a
2.	b	7.	c
3.	d	8.	b
4.	a	9.	c
5.	d	10.	a

INDEX

About the Author

Jon Marthaler writes about soccer for NorthernPitch.com. He will never forget Eric Wynalda's free-kick goal against Switzerland in the 1994 World Cup. He lives in St. Paul, Minnesota, with his wife.